SO-AWU-159

# five cents worth

Lee Aucoin, *Creative Director*
Jamey Acosta, *Senior Editor*
Heidi Fiedler, *Editor*
Produced and designed by
Denise Ryan & Associates
Illustration © Mike Artell
Rachelle Cracchiolo, *Publisher*

**Teacher Created Materials**

5301 Oceanus Drive
Huntington Beach, CA 92649-1030
http://www.tcmpub.com
**Paperback: ISBN: 978-1-4333-5642-1**
**Library Binding: ISBN: 978-1-4807-1741-1**
© 2014 Teacher Created Materials

Written by
Helen Shaw
and Robert Shaw

Illustrated by
Mike Artell

# five cents worth

**Setting:** Two doctors see patients at an Ear, Nose, and Throat Clinic.

| **Scene One** | **Characters** |
|---|---|
| | Nurse Stitch |
| | Nurse Payne |
| | Mr. Spotswood |

| **Scene Two** | **Characters** |
|---|---|
| | Nurse Tend |
| | Dr. Bandage |
| | Dr. Plaster |
| | Ms. Ceylon |
| | Nurse Treat |
| | Nurse Fit |
| | Mrs. Mildew |

## Scene Three

**Characters**

Dr. Bandage
Ms. Depp
Dr. Plaster
Nurse Strong
Nurse Well

## Scene Four

**Characters**

Dr. Bandage
Dr. Plaster
Mr. Rudolf
Nurse Ward
Nurse Hurt

## Scene Five

**Characters**

Mrs. Ripened
Dr. Bandage
Dr. Plaster
Nurse Limp
Nurse Back
Ms. Ceylon
Mrs. Mildew
Ms. Depp
Mr. Rudolf

# Contents

# Scene one

*(A waiting room, two nurses enter.)*

**Nurse Stitch:** My tooth is aching, so I have
a dental appointment today.

**Nurse Payne:** At what time?

**Nurse Stitch:** At tooth-hurty, of course.

**Nurse Payne:** Why did Dr. Croak tell me to walk past the pill cupboard quietly?

**Nurse Stitch:** So you wouldn't wake the sleeping pills.

**Nurse Stitch:** Call Dr. Stump and tell her to go to the Emergency Room immediately.

*(An alarm sounds.)*

**Nurse Payne:** The Emergency Room? What is that?

**Nurse Stitch:** It's a big room with very sick people in it.

*(Mr. Spotswood approaches the nurses.)*

**Nurse Stitch:** What seems to be the trouble, sir?

**Mr. Spotswood:** I keep seeing spots.

**Nurse Stitch:** Have you seen a doctor?

**Mr. Spotswood:** No, just spots.

**Nurse Stitch:** Well, you will need to see the eye doctor then. Just up the stairs, and follow the spots.

*(Mr. Spotswood exits.)*

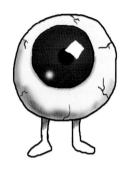

# Scene Two

*(The doctors see more patients.)*

**Nurse Tend:** Doctor, there is a man in the waiting room with a glass eye called Mr. Brown.

**Doctor Bandage:** What does he call his other eye? *(Nurse shrugs and exits.)*

(*Two doctors stop in front of a patient.*)

**Ms. Ceylon:** My right eye hurts whenever I drink tea.

**Doctor Plaster:** Take the spoon out of the mug so it won't poke you.

(*The doctors move on to another patient.*)

**Doctor Plaster:** Now, here's an interesting patient who thinks she is invisible.

**Doctor Bandage:** Sorry, I can't see her right now. I'm having trouble with my eyes.

**Doctor Plaster:** What's wrong?

**Doctor Bandage:** I just can't see myself finding a cure for her.

**Doctor Plaster:** Is she thinking straight? (*To the patient*) Which is closer, Massachusetts or the moon?

**Ms. Ceylon:** The moon, of course. You can't see Massachusetts from here.

**Doctor Bandage:** Did you try wearing your glasses as I suggested?

**Ms. Ceylon:** They didn't work. They made me see-sick.

**Doctor Bandage:** She's fine, not like another patient of mine who thought he was a moth.

**Doctor Plaster:** What did you do?

**Doctor Bandage:** I turned out all the lights and he went looking for a street lamp.

*(Nurses enter.)*

**Nurse Treat:** What do you have if your head is hot, your feet are cold, and you see spots in front of your eyes?

**Nurse Fit:** A polka-dotted sock over your head.

*(Nurses exit.)*

*(Doctors move on to another patient.)*

**Doctor Bandage:** When does it hurt?

**Mrs. Mildew:** When I touch my head *(touches head)*, when I touch my shoulder *(touches shoulder)*, and when I touch my arm *(touches arm)*.

**Doctor Plaster:** You have a broken finger.

OUCH

13

Doctor Bandage: I have the results of the X-ray.

Mrs. Mildew: What is it?

Doctor Bandage: A big complicated image sent to me from the X-ray Department. As you can see, the finger is broken here, here, and here. What would you do in a case like this?

Doctor Plaster: I'd say, "Ouch!"

Doctor Bandage: This woman's finger has been broken in three places.

Doctor Plaster: She shouldn't go to those places again!

Doctor Bandage: I wonder how she feels about this.

Doctor Plaster: Feeling anything is probably painful with a broken finger.

# Scene Three

*(Both doctors move on to another patient.)*

**Doctor Bandage:** I hear you've come here because you can't hear.

**Ms. Depp:** Only when I cough.

**Doctor Bandage:** *(to Doctor Plaster)*
Why didn't she come earlier?

**Doctor Plaster:** She wasn't allowed.

**Doctor Bandage:** Her cough was too loud.
She was disturbing all the other patients.

**Doctor Plaster:** *(Holding hands against the
patient's ear, measuring)* This patient's ear
is 12 inches long.

**Doctor Bandage:** It can't be an ear then.
That makes it a foot.

*(Nurses enter.)*

**Nurse Strong:** Yesterday, I had to bandage
a patient's ears. He was ironing his shirt
when the phone rang and he answered
the iron instead of the phone.

**Nurse Well:** What happened to the other ear?

**Nurse Strong:** They called back.

*(Nurses exit.)*

# Scene Four

*(The doctors meet with more patients.)*

**Doctor Bandage:** My last patient complained that her nose was running and her feet smelled.

**Doctor Plaster:** She was made upside down?

**Doctor Bandage:** Absolutely.

**Doctor Plaster:** Hey there.  So you think you're a snowman?

**Mr. Rudolf:** *(Sniff, sniff)* Can't you smell the carrots?

**Doctor Plaster:** *(to Doctor Bandage)*  He's a serious case.

**Doctor Bandage:** Not to be sneezed at.

**Doctor Plaster:** Is there a sniff of a cure?

**Doctor Bandage:** I've scent for medicine.

**Mr. Rudolf:** *(Grabbing his nose)* Oh no, those pesky rabbits have stolen my nose.

**Doctor Plaster:** How will he smell?

*(Both doctors hold their noses, and invite the audience to join in.)*

**Both Doctors:** TERRIBLE!

**Mr. Rudolf:** When will I get another nose?

Doctor Bandage: It's difficult to tell.

**Mr. Rudolf:** Can't you take a guess?

Doctor Bandage: Well...not for about four weeks.

**Mr. Rudolf:** Can't you guess sooner than that?

*(Nurses enter.)*

**Nurse Ward:** What did the right eye say to the left eye?

**Nurse Hurt:** Just between you and me, something smells!

25

# Scene Five

*(The doctors continue trying to help patients.)*

**Mrs. Ripened:** Doctor, every time I eat fruit, I get a strange urge to give people all my money.

**Doctor Bandage:** Have an apple or a banana. Have both! I'm happy to take your money!

**Mrs. Ripened:** Doctor, is it possible to get a disease from biting insects?

**Doctor Bandage:** Well, yes it is, so I would advise you to stop biting them. Does your tongue burn when you eat chili?

**Mrs. Ripened:** I don't know. I've never tried to light it on fire.

**Doctor Bandage:** I don't think you're eating properly.

**Mrs. Ripened:** But yesterday, I ate a whole sheep!

**Doctor Plaster:** How do you feel?

**Mrs. Ripened:** Baaa-d. Oh, and Doctor, I was caught eating bullets at work.

**Doctor Bandage:** What happened?

**Mrs. Ripened:** I got fired. *(Pause)* Anyway, the food in this hospital tastes funny.

**Doctor Plaster:** That can't be true. You aren't laughing.

**Doctor Bandage:** Did you take the medicine I gave you?

**Mrs. Ripened:** No, the label on the bottle said, "Keep tightly closed."

**Doctor Plaster:** You look very tired.

**Mrs. Ripened:** Yes, the label also said, "Shake before using."

**Doctor Bandage:** Enough! I'm a doctor, but I don't have the patience.

**Mrs. Ripened:** Well, I'm a patient, but I can't wait around all day.

*(Nurses enter.)*

**Nurse Limp:** How does a frog feel when it has a broken leg?

**Nurse Back:** Unhoppy!

*(Nurses exit, limping.)*

**Ms. Ceylon:** *(Points to spot on floor.)* That looks like a banana peel.

**Mrs. Mildew:** *(Bends down and touches the same spot)* That feels like a banana peel.

**Ms. Depp:** *(Cups hand around ear.)* It sounds like a banana peel.

**Mr. Rudolf:** *(Bends down and sniffs.)* It smells like a banana peel.

**Mrs. Ripened:** *(Pretends to touch the spot, then licks finger)* It tastes like a banana peel.

**All:** It's a good thing we didn't slip on it!

*(Nurses enter, limping.)*

**30**

**Nurse Back:** How many cents are there in a nickel?

**Both Doctors:** Seeing, touching, hearing, smelling, and tasting...

**All:** That's what you get for five cents!

**Helen Shaw** and **Robert Shaw** live in Hobart, Tasmania, the island state of Australia. In between writing stories about things that would make life more interesting if they were true, they tell each other jokes that only they think are funny. They live with a very old cat who thinks all of this is extremely silly. *Five Cents Worth* is their first book for Read! Explore! Imagine! Fiction Readers.

**Mike Artell** lives in Covington, near New Orleans, Louisiana. Mike is an award-winning children's book author, illustrator, and TV cartoonist. He is also a musician who plays guitar, keyboard, and blues harmonica. Mike's book *Petit Rouge* was named by the National Association of Elementary School Principals as its 2009 Read Aloud Book of the Year. *Five Cents Worth* is his first book for Read! Explore! Imagine! Fiction Readers.